This book belongs to

. . . .

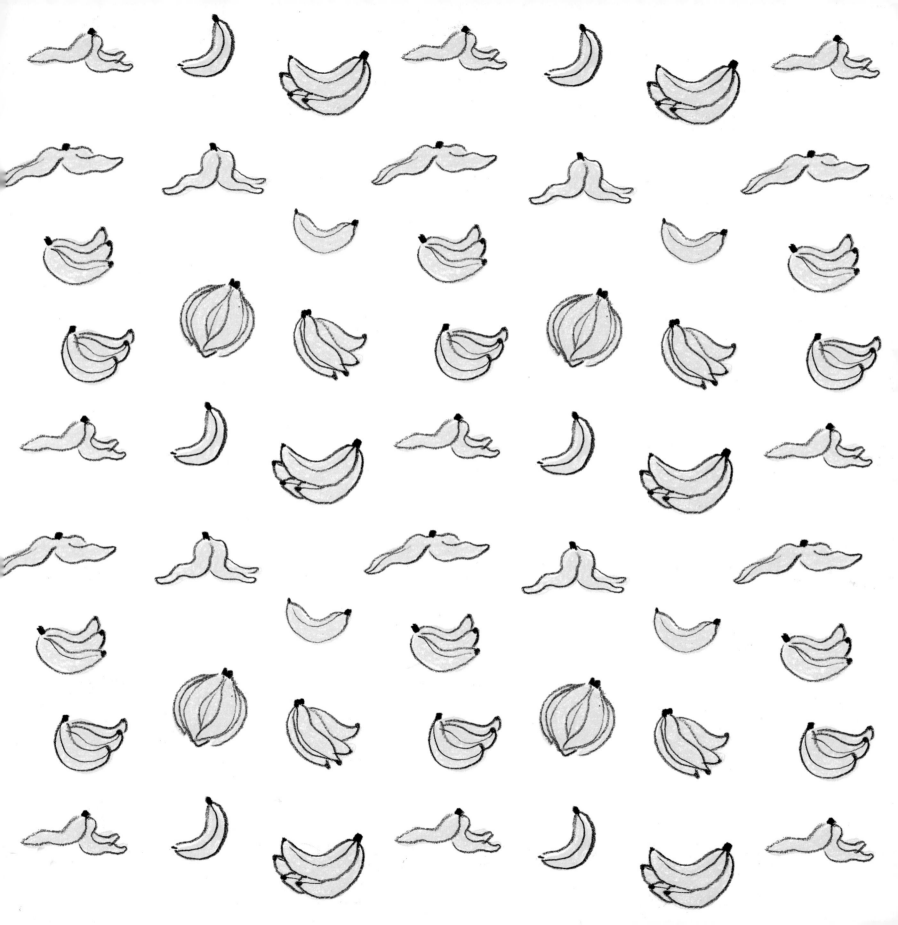

For my niece, Jess

OXFORD
UNIVERSITY PRESS

Great Clarendon Street, Oxford, OX2 6DP,
United Kingdom

Oxford University Press is a department of the University of Oxford.
It furthers the University's objective of excellence in research,
scholarship, and education by publishing worldwide. Oxford is a
registered trade mark of Oxford University Press in the UK and in
certain other countries

Database right Oxford University Press (maker)

First Edition published in 2014

British Library Cataloguing in Publication Data available

ISBN: 978-0-19-273815-8 (hardback)
ISBN: 978-0-19-273816-5 (paperback)

1 3 5 7 9 10 8 6 4 2

Printed in China

Paper used in the production of this book is a natural, recyclable
product made from wood grown in sustainable forests.
The manufacturing process conforms to the environmental
regulations of the county of origin.

Betty
goes bananas

Steve Antony

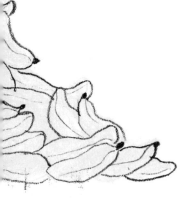

OXFORD
UNIVERSITY PRESS

Betty was hungry.
She saw a banana.
She wanted to eat it.

But the banana . . .

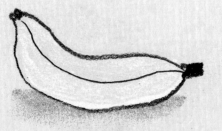

would not open.

Betty tried using
her hands,

and her teeth,

and even her feet,

then suddenly . . .

she calmed down.

'There is no need for that,'
said Mr Toucan.

'Watch. I will show you how to peel the banana.'

Mr Toucan showed Betty how to peel the banana.

But the banana . . .

was Betty's and SHE wanted to peel it.

Betty looked at the banana,

and looked at Mr Toucan,

and looked at the banana again,

then suddenly...

she calmed down.

'There is no need for that,'
said Mr Toucan.

'You can peel the banana the next time you have one.'

Betty started
to eat
the banana.

But the banana . . .

broke!

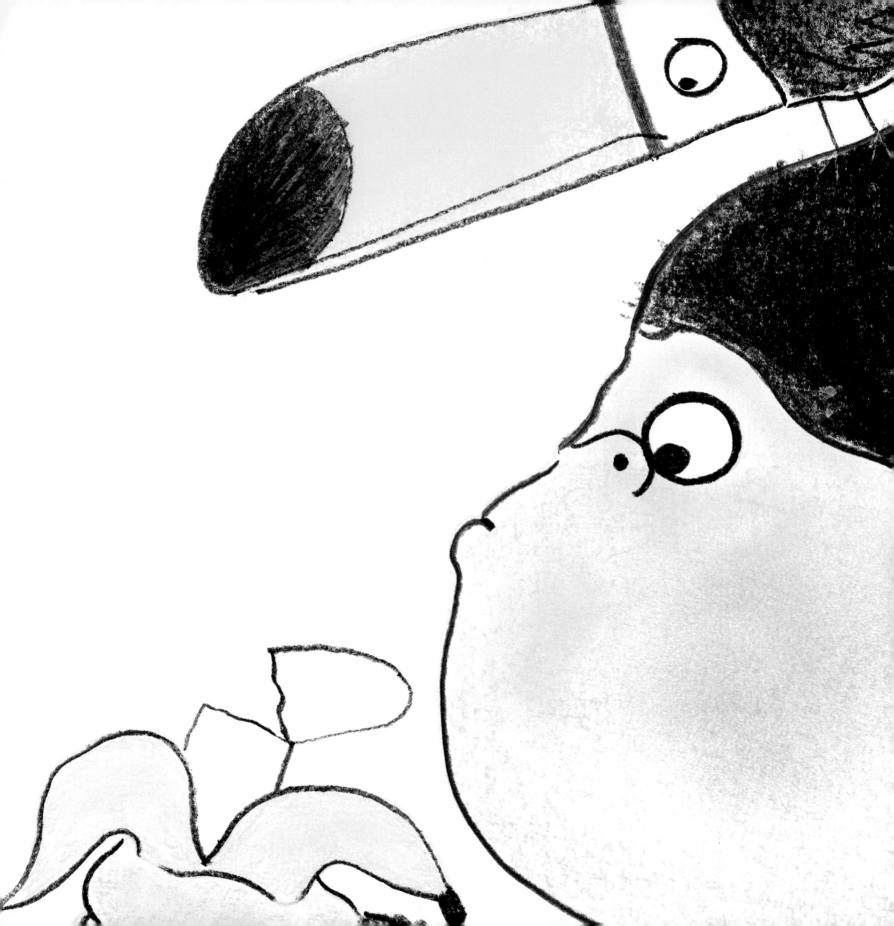

Betty cried,

WAAAAAA!

and sniffled,

SNIFFLE! SNIFF!
SNIFF!

she calmed down.

'There is no need for that,' said Mr Toucan.
'Or would you like ME to have the banana?'

Betty ate the banana . . .

and the banana was

DELICIOUS!

YUM!

Then suddenly . . .

Betty saw another banana . . .

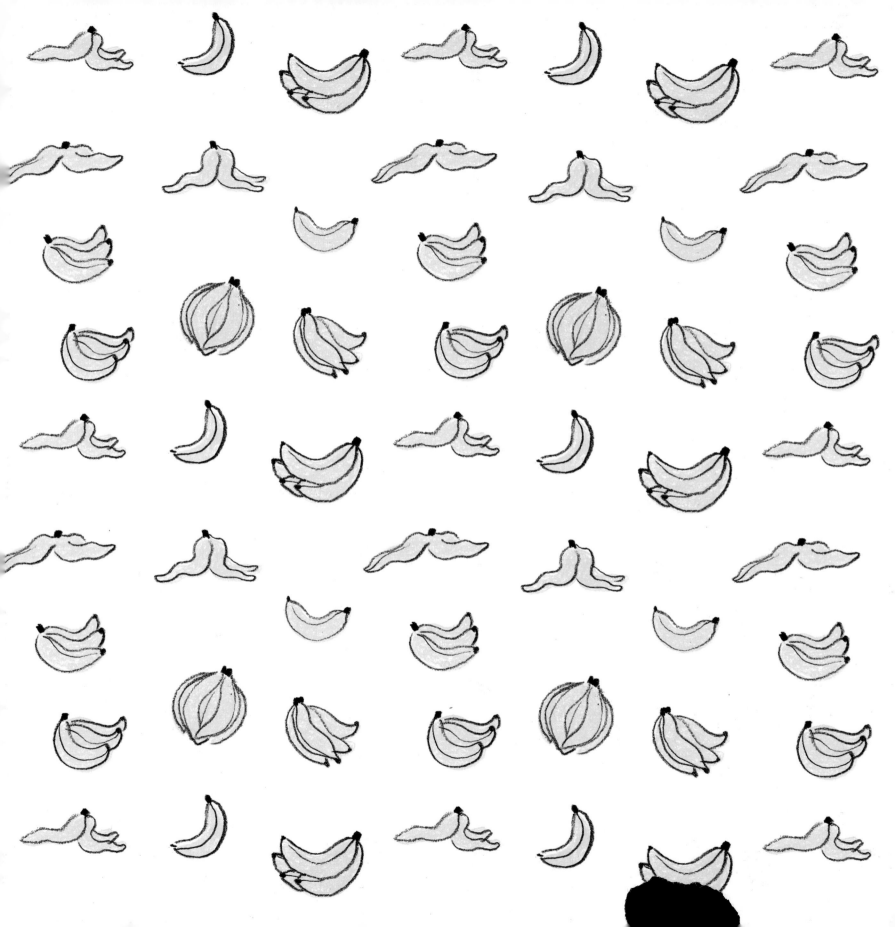